The Haunting

©2019 by Carrie Bates

All rights reserved. No part of this may be reproduced, distributed or transmitted in any form or by any means without prior written permission.

This is a work of fiction. Names, characters, places and incidents are a product of the author's imagination. Any resemblance to actual people, living or dead, or to businesses, events or locales is completely coincidental.

Prologue

Chapter 1

Chapter 2

Chapter 3

Chapter 4

Chapter 5

Chapter 6

Chapter 7

Chapter 8

Chapter 9

Epilogue

More Haunted House Books

Prologue

Emily liked the train most days. She liked the ride from Green Hills where she worked as a maid in three different houses, big houses. The twenty-five cents per hour was a nickel more than some maids earned in other parts of the city. Of course, she didn't get a quarter for every hour she worked. Just the first four; after that, she ran errands and performed little jobs for free. Those were standard work rules in 1920; all the other maids said so. Not that Emily spent much time with other maids. None of the other girls rode the same train. Emily met them in the markets or post office.

And while the girls came from different parts of the area and wore different clothes, they all complained the same. Too much work for too little money. Emily groused with them, but she was still thankful for the work. Her mother earned little as a sewing machine operator, turning out shirtwaists by the thousands. Emily's earnings were vital for the well-being of the household that included her two younger sisters. Mary was almost old enough to look for work herself, but Jane seemed a bit slow. Emily wondered if Jane would ever be able to work.

Emily pushed Jane's troubles out of her head and thought about Christmas, which was only two weeks away. While Emily gave most of her money to her mother, she had kept the little bonus money she received from her employers. She planned to use that money to buy gifts for her sisters and mother. Of course, Emily wanted to spend a little on herself. There was a small gold locket that she had already purchased. The blue velvet box was safe in the bottom of her purse. But she felt the need to pull it out and look at it. As she opened the box, she smiled. There was a little filigree on the cover, something delicate, and it thrilled her. She touched it with her finger … so pretty. She opened the locket and smiled at her initials etched into the gold. Someday, she hoped to fill the locket with a photo of a child.

When she looked up, she noticed the man down the car. He stared at her with an intensity she found discomfiting. She quickly closed the locket and the box and returned it to the bottom of her purse. It was precious.

Outside, snow blew around on a stiff wind. Emily could feel the cold seeping through the window like some kind of frigid animal, trying to steal the warmth from her fingers and nose. The snow was another reason Emily liked the train that saved her the long walk to her home in Oak Bottom. On a cold December night like this, the walk would have been brutal. She shivered, despite the meager heat in the railway car, or maybe because of it. The cold reminded her of the dilapidated house where she lived with her mother and sisters. With a stiff wind, the house would be freezing. There was coal enough for the stove, but the heat didn't seem to drift far away from the stove. Emily was certain that on this night, they would all sleep close to the stove. It was the only way.

The conductor wandered through the car, calling out the name of the next stop - Carbaro. Emily liked the conductor. He seemed like a friend, as she saw him three times a week. Every once in a while, he would let her ride for free, which was a big deal to Emily. Every nickel counted. The conductor smiled at her, and she smiled back. At fifteen, she wasn't yet ready for marriage, but she had her eye out. While the potbellied conductor wasn't on her horizon, she kept her eye on some of the young men who lived in Green Hills. If she got lucky … She didn't finish the thought as the train came to a stop, and everyone left—except for the intense man. That he didn't leave surprised Emily. She knew every one of the seven families who lived at the end of the line. The intense man didn't live in any of those seven houses.

The conductor passed, going in the opposite direction. "Not much longer," he said with a smile.

Emily smiled back, and for a moment, wondered if she should move to another car. Then, she told herself not to be silly. The ride would end soon, and she would be rid of the intense man whose stare she didn't like.

The train started with a jerk, and Emily turned to the window, staring at the blowing snow. She wasn't going to enjoy her walk home. She was still looking when the hand clamped over her mouth and a strong arm wrapped around her.

"Don't make a sound," the man hissed in her ear. "Hand over the purse, and I won't hurt you."

Emily didn't for a moment want to hand over her purse, her money, her locket. She had worked too hard. She had spent too many hours on hands and knees. She held onto her purse and squirmed. She managed to open her mouth. She couldn't scream, but she could bite.

The man yelped and jerked back his hand, losing a piece of flesh. Even as she spit out the filthy part of his hand, she glimpsed the closed fist flying at her. The punch caught her in the middle of her face, and pain shot up her nose. Blinking, Emily tried to think. She suddenly felt sluggish and weak. The next punch caught her cheek, and she heard something snap. More pain shot into her head. A blackness filled her vision.

"Gimme that, you little whore."

She heard the words, but they didn't really register. Still, she told herself to hang onto the purse, her purse, her money, her locket. The purse jerked in her hands. Yet she held on, focusing all her strength on her grip. Her vision was starting to clear when the next blow hit her mouth. She felt her chapped lips split. She knew immediately that blood was running down her chin, that a tooth had been knocked into her mouth.

The blackness narrowed her vision. She was suddenly wondering why she couldn't see. Oh, she remembered. She was being punched … hard.

"You're a feisty one," the man hissed.

For a moment, she felt the tug on the purse slacken. *What?*

The punch hit her in the neck, and her head rocked. Hands pried her fingers open, and her purse, her precious purse, was ripped away.

Her head exploded with pain, and a small scream escaped her mouth. That caused the man to stuff something in her mouth. She didn't know what it was. She knew only that she couldn't breathe as her nose was broken and swollen. She tried to breathe. She tried to pull the cloth from her mouth, but strangely, her hands wouldn't obey her brain. She couldn't find her mouth. She couldn't find anything.

She more heard the window going up than saw it. The rush of cold air felt good on her face, but why was the window open? She kept trying to pull the cloth from her mouth. She fought the darkness that was stealing away her sight.

"Out you go," the man said. "And you deserve worse."

Emily knew she was being lifted off the seat, but she couldn't quite fathom why. In a second, her feet and legs were out in the cold, and that felt almost right, almost. Then, the rest of her followed, and she found herself falling. Her head hit the frozen ground, and a blast of light and pain shot through her brain. She couldn't see. She couldn't breathe. She tried to move, but nothing seemed to work. Not that she quite remembered why she was lying on the frozen ground. The darkness deepened as a new pain from her leg arrived at her brain. She found that almost amusing. So much pain from so many places. She tried to remember what had caused the commotion.

Oh yes, her purse.

She felt with her fingers.

No purse.

Where …

The darkness took away everything, leaving Emily lying on the hard ground.

The conductor stood on the platform, waiting for the final two passengers to disembark. The stranger came first. Hat pulled down over his face, sullen and silent; he passed without a word. As far as the conductor was concerned that was just about right. He had no love for the misfits who sometimes rode the train.

Where was Emily?

The conductor knew she was on the train, and this was her stop, the last one. He waited a minute before he boarded the train to look. He walked the length of the train. He didn't find her. He didn't think she had slipped past him, but that had to be explanation. No way she was going to jump from a moving train. He shook his head and went to tell the engineer to take the train back to the terminal. Emily didn't often leave without a word, but it seemed this night, she had.

The conductor was too busy with paperwork to look out the window on the trip back to the terminal. If he had looked, he might have spotted Emily's broken body being slowly covered by the bitter snow.

Chapter 1

Debra Barnes finished sealing the last box. She set it atop the others against the wall, and for the thousandth time since she contemplated the move, she asked herself if she was doing the right thing. Oak Bottom didn't sound like a place she would find hospitable, and yet, she knew the small town was smack-dab in the middle of the furniture-making capital of the country. A small furniture and décor store in Oak Bottom would have very short supply lines. She would be able to fulfill orders in days, not weeks. And she would have access to the best furniture designers and manufacturers in the country. It was a no-brainer. Well, it would have been a no-brainer if Todd were still around.

She jumped onto the breakfast bar and sat, wondering just how things between her and Todd had gone so wrong. Everything had started so well. Love, sex, laughs; they'd had it all. Well, she'd had it all. For some reason, Todd hadn't felt the same way. After only two years of living together, he'd announced that he was moving out.

Where?

He wouldn't say, and that stung Debra more than anything. He didn't trust her enough to tell her where he was going. As she had watched him walk away, she'd reminded herself that she had agreed to the cohabitation agreement. If she had assumed that it would dovetail into something else, well, that was her problem, not his. While she had shed her fair share of tears after he left, she kept reminding herself that she had made the bargain. If it was a bad one, that was her fault. Yet she couldn't remain where she was. If one dream had to be abandoned, another one had to take its place. Oak Bottom would be that dream. She would employ what she had learned about décor and furniture and own that small place her heart had always wanted. And who knew what might happen? Perhaps, just perhaps, Oak Bottom might supply someone or something that would bring joy to her heart again. It had to be better than moping around.

Oak Bottom.

The name didn't sound like much, but she had done some research. The town had grown from a handful of houses in the roaring twenties to a respectable number of homes of various sizes. Furthermore, Oak Bottom was the end of a railroad line that started in the heart of the city. The depot had recently been renovated, adding a shopping area consisting of small retail stores and restaurants beneath the platform. One of those small stores would be hers. Not only would the residents of Oak Bottom be her customers, but the train would bring a richer clientele from the city. That Oak Bottom also featured one of the best-known horror museums in the country was an even bigger plus. A raft of tourists would amble by her shop. Certainly, some of them would like a curio or two to mark their time in Oak Bottom.

She looked across the room at the stack of boxes. Her furniture had already been shipped. It was on a truck somewhere between where she sat and Oak Bottom. She had managed to secure one of the original houses in Oak Bottom. Over a hundred years old, the house was drafty and filled with creaks and squeaks and squeals. Debra knew this from the two visits she had made before buying the place. It was her house now, and the contents of the boxes would soon fill the cabinets and bureaus in her new house. That made her feel a little better. Todd would soon be nothing more than a passing memory.

She hoped.

Chapter 2

Debra placed the last Dracula doll on the shelf and stepped back to admire her goods. Dracula had joined Frankenstein and several zombies in this corner of her new store. They were tributes to the horror museum not far away, and she hoped the dolls would appeal to the children who would arrive via train to visit the museum. They were not particularly scary dolls, which was fine with Debra. The last thing she wanted was to frighten a child. The world was too frightening a place the way it was. If she added newer horror figures, she risked losing the innocent segment of her customers. Of course, Dracula was no match for a cuddly teddy bear, but there might be a place for him on a bookshelf.

She grabbed the empty box and looked around her new store. Tomorrow was the big day, opening day, and she wanted everything to look exactly right. She had divided the store into sections. The horror museum corner had been stocked with not just dolls but DVDs and some board games. She knew that board games were no match for computer games, but she was hoping to appeal to parents who wanted to limit the time their children spent in front of a small backlit screen. The games were family oriented, and who didn't want a game the entire family could play? With the games came the theme keychains. Add Frankenstein or Dracula to keys. Maybe they wouldn't get lost so often—just at night. She chuckled at the thought.

Another corner featured the small wooden doodads and household items that came from local sources. The typical plaques that made fun of Oak Bottom or "Oak Butt" as the locals liked to call it. Added to the plaques and signs were wooden spoons, decorative bowls, and a small section dedicated to oak paper towel holders and spice racks. She wasn't trying to compete with the big kitchen and bath stores, but all her items were handmade and durable. She guessed they would appeal to a certain clientele. She particularly liked the oak-framed calendar which she thought looked terrific, so terrific she had added it to her own kitchen. Her calendar had a big red ring around it for opening day.

One wall was dedicated to books. She had put out a call for local authors who wanted a platform for their cookbooks, novels, and histories of Oak Bottom. Again, Debra was using local sources and one-of-a-kind items. To her surprise and delight, she had found the area fully stocked with dedicated and competent writers who were only too happy to join her enterprise. There was even a book about local paranormal activity. Oak Bottom was no Amityville, but it seemed there were a few odd occurrences in the neighborhood. Debra had promised herself to read the book so she could better converse with the customers from the horror museum. Steering them to a spooky house or whispering well might just bring a sale.

    She had added a jewelry case at the last minute, and that was where her register and credit card connection were. She hadn't been sold on the jewelry in the beginning, but the horror- themed charm bracelets and amulets seemed too good to pass up. To keep from becoming nothing more than a horror shop, she had added a whimsical collection of unicorns and fairies. She didn't fathom why things that couldn't be seen were such a hit with people of all ages, but they were; perhaps because reality wasn't all that great or comforting. Best of all was that the jewelry sparkled inside the case. It drew the eye. She hoped it would open wallets and pocketbooks.

Satisfied with her store, with its arrangement and inventory, Debra carried the empty box to the storeroom. It was a small storeroom because she did not wish to carry a lot of inventory. If she ran out of something or had a special request, she knew she could provide the item in days because her suppliers were nearby. The close proximity was a huge advantage. No one wanted to wait weeks for an impulse purchase. While in the storeroom, she checked the rear door, making sure it was securely locked. Since trains didn't run all night, the station would be empty for hours, and in hours, she didn't want to make it easy for any would-be thief.

As she checked the door, the last train left the station. It had arrived minutes before with its load of late arrivals. Debra suspected there were few if any, passengers heading back to the city. The arrivals had no doubt already left the station. She also knew the other shops and one restaurant were closed. Since the shopping area was new, there wasn't a steady flow from Oak Bottom— not that Oak Bottom could provide enough traffic to keep them all in business. Perhaps in time, the restaurant would stay open later. Debra wasn't at all sure she wanted to be open late on the off chance some half-drunk shopper wanted a Dracula doll.

As she shut off the lights, she felt a pang of anxiety. For the thousandth time, she asked herself if she was doing the right thing. Opening her shop was a huge gamble. Oak Bottom was a mammoth risk. If the store failed, she could always find a way to stay afloat, but it would take years to recoup the losses. Worse, she would forever consider herself a failure. She wasn't at all sure her psyche could take the hit. Standing in the middle of her shop, her merchandise, she shivered. *With huge risk came huge opportunity* … That was what she had to focus on: opportunity. This was the opportunity she had been seeking for a long time. She had the chance to succeed and enjoy her life. Hard work? No doubt, but she promised herself that she would make it pay.

Debra set the alarm and quickly locked the front door. She knew the local police would drive through the parking lot every hour or so, but they wouldn't patrol on foot unless they suspected some kind of criminal activity. Good locks were tantamount. Checking the door, she turned from the shop and started away from the escalator that had already automatically stopped running. No need to run the escalator to the platform with no arrivals or departures.

That was when she spotted the girl.

The girl was young, a teenager. At least, she looked like a teen to Debra. And the girl was oddly dressed, which was what struck Debra right off. Halloween was just around the corner, so Debra expected a jacket of some kind, but the girl wore a coat, a winter coat, and even from a distance, Debra could tell that the coat was worn. In fact, the coat looked old. Well, not exactly old; the coat had a style that wasn't current. It looked like something girls wore decades before. Modern girls wore all manner of ski jackets and coats that looked more like pillows than coats. But this girl's black coat was plain. Flat. It was odd, but then, Oak Bottom was odd as far as Debra was concerned. As she approached the girl, Debra noticed that not just the coat was odd, but so was the shoe.

Shoe.

That was the first anomaly Debra noticed about the girl's feet. She wore but one shoe. And that shoe was more of a boot, over the ankle, and buttoned down the front.

Buttons.

Debra didn't know of any girl who still wore button shoes. But there were some trendy types who featured button or faux button shoes. Fashion magazines were filled with photos of leggy models in button boots - or something. Debra was pretty sure the buttons were for show, hiding a zipper somewhere that did the real work. But the girl's shoe looked authentic as if it required some sort of hook device in order to put the button through the loop. The shoe was as worn as the coat; as old. Debra couldn't help but wonder just what was going on. The dark sock on the shoeless foot matched the coat. The sock had fallen down around the girl's ankle as if the sock had no elastic in it. Did socks even come without elastic anymore? Debra was certain they did, to match button shoes that weren't really button shoes.

Hair.

The girl's long dark hair hung down beside her bowed head, hiding her face. The hair seemed normal, but then, girls had been wearing their hair long forever. It was older women who eschewed long hair for shorter, easier to care for cuts. *The hair needs a good washing* was what Debra thought as she approached her. Why did some girls treat basic hygiene as a "maybe" thing? Being clean was the first step to self-confidence. Debra had learned that as a teenager.

Not that she was going to say anything to the girl. Debra might hint, but she certainly wasn't going into full "mother" mode. It was when she got close that Debra noticed that the girl was crying.

Debra stopped.

The quiet crying was unmistakable. No heaving of the shoulders, no sniffling, no sobs, the girl was simply crying as if she had lost a puppy or kitten. It was the crying of late night when the lights were out, and no one could hear. It was the crying of complete and utter loss. It was the crying of despair, the last refuge of a broken heart or mind. It was a crying that spoke to Debra's heart, for she had come to know the tears that moistened a pillow when the moon was covered by clouds. The girl's sorrow made Debra bite her lip. Debra shared that feeling, that loss. If she hadn't tossed aside the depression, she wouldn't have her own store now. She would be as lost as this young girl.

    Debra knew she had to do something. No feeling person could simply walk past this needy human being. That would be cruel. For some reason, Debra was certain that the girl had no place to go, no warm bed, no hot food, and no one to say a kind word to her. And if Debra had learned anything from her own ordeals, she had learned to reach out as her own best friend had reached out. Had it not been for someone else, Debra might still be wallowing in self-pity. It was amazing what magic a few simple, heartfelt words could work. And she wanted to extend that magic to the girl. *What was the term? Pay it forward? Do a good deed so that the receiver could, in turn, do a good deed?* This was her chance to add a credit to her own life ledger.

Debra approached closer, confident that she could help the weeping girl. There was a bowl of chicken soup waiting for the girl at Debra's new home. It would be simple.

Debra reached out, and as she did, the girl stood. Debra still couldn't see her face, and the girl made no effort to turn. That stopped Debra, and she wondered just what she should do. Then, the dog barked.

The bark caused Debra to turn her head. She looked down the walkway, but there was no dog. What? She had heard it. Where was it? Certainly, it hadn't run away that fast. Shrugging, she turned back.

The girl was gone. Gone?

Debra gasped, completely baffled. She had turned her head for only a few seconds. The girl couldn't have walked away that fast. An Olympic sprinter couldn't have disappeared that fast. And yet, Debra was alone, utterly alone. The girl was gone, vanished without a trace. It seemed impossible, and yet, Debra had to believe her eyes.

Or did she?

Debra faced a conundrum. Either she had seen a girl that could run like a flash, or Debra had imagined the girl altogether. She didn't like to think her brain could conjure up a complete image as real as the girl. Certainly, Debra was tired, but she wasn't fatigued to the point where she was hallucinating. That was beyond the pale. That was the stuff of psychotics. She spun to look in all directions. She even looked up, as if the girl could cling to the ceiling like a spider. But the girl was not there. Had she ever been?

Debra shook her head and wondered, even as she started for her car. Unless she was willing to believe in ghosts, she had to assume she had made the thing up. There had never been a girl. That brought doubt into Debra's mind. If the girl had never been there …

Debra hurried to her car and drove as fast as she could to her house. She didn't like the idea that her brain could be playing tricks. She needed sleep, rest, a way to rid herself of the pressure she was feeling. She poured herself a glass of wine to calm her nerves and took a hot bath. Slipping into bed, she felt much better. She had read about people who occasionally imagined things that weren't there, and often, those people functioned just fine. And if it happened only once, well then, it might as well not have happened at all. That was the last thought Debra had before she closed her eyes.

And heard the girl weeping.

Chapter 3

Debra's eyes popped open, and she looked around her bedroom.

Nothing.

She flipped on the light and looked again.

No one.

Under the covers, Debra shook. She had heard the girl. She knew she had heard the girl. It couldn't be anything but the girl. Debra knew. And yet, there was no girl, no sound, nothing. It was wishful thinking, or maybe not thinking at all. It was a sound in the night, perhaps the house, something that her brain attributed to a girl that couldn't be there. That was it. Debra was suddenly sure that the old house had sighed or hiccupped or something, and she had automatically thought of the girl in the train station; the girl that wasn't there in reality. Crazy but true.

Debra wondered if she was losing her mind. If she didn't have the opening the next day, she might have considered contacting a health professional. But she did have the opening, and it was going to be a huge opening, and when it was over, and she could afford to rest, the weeping girl would disappear. Sleep, Debra needed sleep. She turned off the light and closed her eyes and … listened.

Nothing.

Debra had never been so happy to hear … nothing.

***

The next day dawned clear and cool, and by the time Debra finished breakfast, she had already forgotten about the weeping girl—

mostly. Doubt still occupied a small corner of her brain, but it was a shaded corner, and the doubt was tiny, almost nonexistent. She had had a moment of dissonance, nothing more. As she drove to the train station, she mentally ran through the checklist she had compiled during the weeks leading up to this day. There were a number of tasks to attend to before she unlocked the front door. Yes, she had gone through the tasks several times already in practice, but today was the real deal, show time. She wanted things to go smoothly. She wasn't seeking perfection, for that was probably impossible. Smooth and glitch-free was what she wanted. That would make it a good day.

Walking to the shop, Debra couldn't help but look at the bench where she had seen the girl the night before. The bench was empty, just as Debra expected. No girl, no button shoe, no old coat, no lank hair. Those were images conjured up by her exhausted mind, nothing more. The empty bench made Debra smile. She unlocked her door with a happy step. The day was starting just as planned. In an hour, commuters would arrive as the first train of the day discharged people heading for the museum. Debra would be ready.

And she was ready.

And the shoppers arrived.

And while sales were not overwhelming, they were brisk. That kept her busy answering questions and ringing up sales. That was the best part. She was making money. The tourists and some of the commuters liked the array of merchandise, from the wooden knickknacks to the Dracula dolls. By lunchtime, Debra was feeling both a bit harried and extremely pleased.

There was a minute or two when her credit card connection failed, but that was an act of the telephone company. If that was the worst that happened on opening day, she would be ecstatic. She closed for lunch and walked to the restaurant. A salad and tea in the October sunshine fit her frame of mind. That she looked around for the weeping girl couldn't be helped. Again, Debra saw nothing, and to her great satisfaction, she imagined nothing. She wanted to laugh.

The rest of the day passed as quickly as the morning. She sold and restocked where she could and greeted everyone with a smile. She didn't take a break for dinner, as she wanted to remain open until the last train left the station. She could eat at home, which was cheaper. Toward the end, when traffic had declined, she started counting up her receipts; her take for the day. She was pleased. She had exceeded her expectations if only a little. That meant that if her business continued according to plan, she would be able to hire an employee in a month or two. Someone to share the burden would be a godsend. She didn't know how many seven-day-a-week stints she could handle. She supposed she could consider closing for one day per week, but her income wasn't there yet. She couldn't afford it. But in time, in time, she could.

She listened for the last train to pull out, for the last passenger to amble past. Then she turned off her lights and gathered her receipts for the day. She would finish the paperwork at home. There was no reason to hang around the store. As she locked the front door, she forced herself not to look for the weeping girl. For some insane reason, she didn't want to check. But, of course, she had to check as she turned for the parking lot.

The bench was empty.

No girl, no button shoe, no coat, no lank hair.

Debra grinned. The doubt in the far corner of her brain grew even smaller. She was certain that the entire episode had been nothing more than a mental glitch, some image culled from some book she had read as a teenager. Déjà vu. *Didn't people remember things they had never seen? Didn't they relive what they had read? Wasn't that why children played pirate or Indiana Jones?* She wanted to laugh.

The drive home proved uneventful, and Debra was more than pleased. Dinner and wine accompanied the posting of her first day of business in her online accounting system. For now, she was also the bookkeeper and sole employee, and it gave her a great deal of satisfaction to recognize that she was in the black already—for a day. She didn't know what the next day would bring, but for one day, she was profitable. She was a success. For one day, she could banish the doubt and angst. She had made it. She was living the dream.

She laughed. What a dream.

Alone in her bedroom, the lights off, she closed her eyes and waited for the weeping girl.

No, not this night, not this time. The room was silent. She could hear the ticking of the windup clock on the bureau. That was a welcome sound. That meant her night should remain undisturbed. She settled down in the bed and let sleep overwhelm her. She didn't think she would dream, at least, not a dream that she would remember. And she was right.

***

The second day began like the first, but then, it broke down a bit. A woman's child managed to snap a wooden spoon, and while Debra wasn't looking, someone managed to make off with a wooden-handled umbrella. As it was raining, she supposed the person needed the umbrella, but she was sickened by the fact that it had been stolen. She hated the idea of people taking her valuable goods. She was resigned to losing a certain percentage because that was the way of the world. Her store wouldn't be the lone beacon of perfect honesty; that was impossible. But on only the second day? While she might have wanted to cry, she didn't. She was too busy. And if the umbrella was the only item she lost in the first week, she would be ahead of the game.

Closing time stirred a little anxiety inside her. The small doubt still clinging to her brain tried to jump to the fore and make a fuss, but she tamped it down. This night, she didn't hide her eyes from the bench. She looked right at it.

No buttons, no coat, no lank hair, no weeping.

Debra was once again sure of her first diagnosis—imagination fueled by fatigue. She shook her head and started for the car, she had books to keep, and a glass of wine to enjoy. And she did enjoy it. In her bed, she listened yet one more night. The house greeted her with its usual creaks and cracks, but there was no weeping. The clock was silent, which reminded her that it needed winding. But she wasn't leaving her warm bed for that. It could wait. Routine. After only a few days, her life was already settling down into a routine. That was a good thing. Debra knew that life consisted of habits, and good habits were hard to anchor. Her new life would be filled with good habits. She was committed to that. Now, she simply had to add the winding of the clock to her other good habits.

***

For the next two weeks, Debra trimmed and sculpted her routine. She dropped the unnecessary items she had originally put on her to-do list and added some necessary ones. The flow of customers proved steady, and the sales of the dolls and other Halloween goods picked up. She was amazed by what people bought in order to celebrate the last day of the month. It seemed that every other person wanted something ghostly or ghoulish, which was fine with her. The more she sold, the better she felt. And all her items sold. Well, maybe not some of the high-end things. She knew those awaited just the right shopper. They weren't for everyone. She was pleasantly surprised by the museum visitors. It seemed her goods were cheaper than the museum gift shop. She hadn't planned on that, but it was good to know. While the weather turned colder and wetter, she watched as the days shortened, and the leaves turned colors. October was a good month as far as she was concerned. It certainly beat the drab gray of winter.

A few days before Halloween, Debra put out a dish of candy, something for shoppers to take while they browsed. She knew it was a good investment. People who got something free often bought something in return. They didn't have to, but there was a fairness about the exchange. And the kids loved to pull something out of the bowl. Parents didn't always allow their kids to eat the candy immediately, which was fine with Debra. She found no joy in picking up empty wrappers around the store. Let the urchins eat the candy on the train.

It was the night before Halloween, and Debra had stayed open a few minutes longer than usual, just in case someone wanted a gift for some masquerade party he or she had to attend. As she locked up, she felt a bit more tired than usual. The ramp up to the holiday had kept her busy, and while she liked the money, she knew she needed a bit more rest. In a way, she was happy that the holiday would soon pass. Of course, that meant she would have to restock with Pilgrims and turkeys and Thanksgiving fare, but that could be done over a few days. And she suspected that the worsening weather would cut down the number of shoppers. Weather was weather. The museum wouldn't be crowded again until the Christmas season hit. In fact, Debra thought it might be a good idea to add the Christmas items to the Thanksgiving ones. That made sense since she knew the big stores were going to do the same thing.

Checking the bench for the weeping girl had become part of Debra's routine, and this night was no different. She looked the bench over and was pleased to find it empty. Then, for some reason she couldn't quite fathom, she looked at the still escalators. That was when she saw her.

Debra saw the weeping girl slowly climbing up the escalator, one step at a time, one shoe on, one shoe off.

Chapter 4

Debra couldn't believe her eyes. She blinked and shook her head and looked again. Nothing had changed. The weeping girl, the exact same girl, was slowly moving up the escalator. It was more than uncanny. It was unbelievable. As Debra watched, she began to shake. The little demon at the back of her brain danced and giggled with delight. Hadn't it told her that the girl was real? Well, if not real, then certainly proof that Debra was losing her mind. Hadn't it warned her?

Debra hesitated another moment before she began to move.

"Hey," Debra called. "Wait!"

But the weeping girl didn't wait. She continued to climb with that hesitant gait. It was as if she hadn't heard Debra. Certainly, Debra was being ignored. Debra hurried, trying to catch up. As she reached the bottom of the escalator, she saw the weeping girl turn the corner to the platform. In a way, that pleased Debra. There were no trains to take and no place to hide on the platform. Unless the weeping girl jumped down on the tracks, she had no place to go. Still, Debra quickly ran up the escalator steps. She wanted to catch up with the girl. Why? Debra wasn't exactly sure, but she felt a need to meet the girl, to talk to her, to find out more about her. No matter how many times Debra reminded herself that the weeping girl was simply a peripheral item, she couldn't convince herself to let go of the girl. Debra needed to know.

At the top of the escalator, Debra turned after the weeping girl. She reached the platform and stopped.

The platform was empty.

At least, it looked empty. There were three benches with advertisement panels where the girl might hide, but the platform *felt* empty. Debra started walking. She had to check the panels, and she had to check the tracks because the weeping girl might well be walking those. But Debra was almost certain she wouldn't see the weeping girl again. That certainty was a gut feeling. As she rounded each and every panel, she found nothing but the latest catchphrase for a soda company and some insurance company logo.

No weeping girl.

Debra reached the end of the platform and went to the edge, looking up and down the track.

No weeping girl.

She looked across the track, where the chain-link fence kept out animals.

Still, no weeping girl.

Baffled and scared, Debra backed away from the platform edge. She looked left and right and again up, but there was no weeping girl, nothing. Debra was alone, utterly alone—except for the cackling voice inside her head that promised that she was going out of her mind. That cackling voice turned her away from the tracks. That voice chased her down the escalator and out to her car. That voice rode in the passenger seat and mocked her.

Was there really a stop sign coming up?

Was the light really green?

Was this really the way home?

She didn't answer the voice, because to answer would give some credence to the voice, some life. She wasn't going to do that. She was going to follow her habits, her routines. She turned there because she always turned there. She parked in the drive because she always parked in the drive. She poured herself a glass of wine because that was her routine. There was safety in routines. There was a damper on the voice in her routines. She drank off the first glass of wine quickly and poured a second.

That wasn't a routine.

But tonight, she felt she needed another glass. The second coming of the weeping girl had unnerved Debra. The second coming had ruptured the cocoon Debra had woven around herself. The trek up the escalator was decidedly not routine. It was part of a world she did not wish to acknowledge as real. Debra felt she was walking along a narrow line. On one side was her normal life, her routine life—up in the morning, off to work, home at night. The other side was the shadowland of weeping girls with one shoe who disappeared shortly after they were spotted. Debra didn't want to cross over the line. She did not want to get stuck in the shadow world, for, in that world, she would talk to a person who wasn't there. Debra would see what no one else saw and hear what no one else heard. The shadow world was an asylum as encompassing as any physical hospital. No, she had to stick to the routine side of the line. And that side said it was time to eat, update the books, and go to bed. That side said there would be no more sightings for this night.

No matter what the mocking voice said. No matter the dreams she had of the weeping girl.

Chapter 5

Debra didn't have to force herself out of her house the next morning, but she certainly wasn't as eager as usual. The weeping girl had unnerved Debra. Well, not the girl so much as her ability to disappear. And that caused the dissonance inside Debra's mind. If the weeping girl were real, then she certainly couldn't just disappear. So, she couldn't be real. Being unreal then, Debra's tired, overworked brain was conjuring up the image, the imagination. In a way, that was far scarier than the weeping girl. If Debra couldn't trust her brain, what could she trust? If she couldn't believe her eyes, what could she believe? She felt as if she had followed Alice down the rabbit hole and into the world of talking animals and crazy queens. In that insane world, nothing was quite right. No pill could be taken with confidence. No one could navigate through Neverland with assurance. It was madness.

When Debra left her parked car, she tried to avoid looking at the benches and escalators, anyplace where the weeping girl might occupy. The last thing she needed was another run in with the lank-haired girl. Debra had a business to run. How would she function if her hands shook and her eyes wouldn't focus?

No weeping girl.

That Debra didn't see the girl was not all that comforting. In a way, she wished the girl was real. If Debra and the girl talked, that would tell Debra that she wasn't losing her mind. That would be a victory of sorts, maybe the best victory. But Debra managed to open her shop and ready her goods without any sign of the girl, without any additional problem with her brain. As shoppers gradually drifted into the store, as they bought porcelain elves and stuffed pilgrims, Debra forgot about the weeping girl and her ability to vanish without leaving a sign. Work and more work proved to be the solution to the weeping girl problem. Even at lunch, Debra was too busy to look too closely for the girl. The needs of the shop overwhelmed everything else. Out of mind … out of sight.

While Debra was just fine during business hours, as she closed her store, her nervousness increased. She knew that the witching hour was drawing near, that moment when she would either succumb to a faulty brain or manage to escape without seeing what couldn't be there. She didn't dare look out the windows. She didn't dare test her mind. She wanted the only things looking back at her when she left the store to be

Santa, his reindeer, and maybe a plastic elf or two. No weeping girl. Nothing that would make Debra doubt herself. She couldn't guarantee that she could control her emotions. What if she spotted the weeping girl again?

Debra didn't answer that question.

After locking the front door, Debra tried to look straight ahead, not really looking up at all. Yet she couldn't stop herself from looking to the benches, from searching for that poor, poor girl.

The benches were empty.

The still escalators were empty.

Debra gave herself a mental pat on the back for being brave as she hurried to her car. She had dared to look. She had dared to test her brain. No weeping girl, no problem inside Debra's head. That made her feel slightly better.

For some crazy reason, Debra felt an uncanny dread as she approached her car. She completely stopped a few feet away and stared. She knew, just knew, that someone was in the back seat. Someone was waiting for Debra to get behind the wheel. Someone was ready to reach around, pull Debra's head back, and whisper evil into Debra's ear. While the parking lot lights were decorated with smiling Santas and elves, something dark and sinister lurked in her car. The feeling was so strong that Debra couldn't get herself to move. She stood and stared, her heart pounding, her lips quivering.

She looked around, hoping to find someone about, someone who would add some courage, some verve.

No one.

Debra was alone, totally alone.

She closed her eyes and gave herself a sermon. There was no one in the car. There was nothing in the car. There was no weeping girl in the dark of the back seat. Debra was making herself scared for absolutely no reason. It was crazy. It was creating self-doubt for no reason. She told herself to grow up and go home. Opening her eyes, she stepped forward and pulled open the rear door.

Empty.

Debra stared and swallowed hard. What was wrong with her mind? Why did she expect something weird for no reason? She slammed the door shut and climbed behind the wheel. As she started the engine, she shook her head in disgust. She was regressing to her childhood, to those nights when she was certain there was a monster under the bed. So sure had she been as a child, she couldn't bring herself to actually look. When was she going to grow up? She started the engine and roared out of the parking lot.

At home, Debra poured a glass of wine and went to work on the books. She pushed the weeping girl and the fear away, angry that so much time had been devoted to feeling afraid. What Debra needed to fear was the loss of her mind, not some image she had resurrected from some book read during adolescence. She chastised herself for being dumb. In bed, she dared to ask out loud for the weeping girl to appear.

Nothing happened; exactly as Debra had expected.

**

Two days passed without any sighting of the weeping girl. Debra believed her justified anger had finally cleared her brain of the image.

All she needed was a good talking to. To give in to fear was to feed it. She would not be so foolish. She was going to end her penchant for scary things.

Outside, icy snow blew past the windows, reminding Debra that it was indeed winter. The weather had curtailed traffic, and Debra considered closing early. But before she could decide, the door opened and a homeless woman entered.

Chapter 6

Debra watched the woman carefully. Not because Debra was afraid the woman would steal something but because the woman looked totally beaten. Debra guessed the woman was perhaps forty, but in her condition, it was hard to tell. She wore a soiled and stained long coat, one of those puffy ones that were filled with filler. The woman's coat had seen better days as the filler had been beaten down in places, making the coat thin in spots. Debra guessed the thin spots were where the woman slept on the sidewalk or against a wall. That the woman needed a shower was evident from the moment the door closed. That the woman was upset was signaled by the way the gloves on her hands shook. As the woman slung a backpack off her shoulders,

Debra wondered if she was about to be robbed for the first time.

"Can I help you?" Debra asked.

"I hope so," the woman answered. "You buy jewelry?" The woman coughed, a deep rasp that spoke to some sort of illness.

"This isn't a pawnshop," Debra answered.

"And I wouldn't sell this to a pawnshop. I was hoping you could see your way to helping me out."

The woman reached into her backpack and removed a blue velvet jewelry box where most of the nap had been rubbed off. She set the box on the counter with a fatalistic air.

"It's the last thing I have that's worth anything, and I, well, I need to get out of Oak Butt. I need to get away."

Debra opened the velvet box. Inside, against a silk lining that was bare with age, was a delicate gold locket and chain. There was a filigree on the locket that gave it a special air.

"May I?" Debra asked and pointed to the locket.

"Go ahead," the woman answered. "It's real gold. And it's old; upwards of a hundred years, I'm guessing."

Debra examined the locket which was indeed gold and in excellent shape. She opened the locket to discover initials etched inside.

"I don't know about the letters," the woman said. "It's always been that way."

Debra was no jeweler, but she recognized quality when she saw it. And she also knew that the locket was something that would have a place in her shop. It would command the jewelry counter and even if she never sold it, the locket would draw people to it.

"You understand that I have to ask," Debra said. "Where did you get this?"

"I knew you were going to want to know," the woman said. "So, I guess I better start at the beginning. That locket came from some long-dead uncle. I don't know which one. Like I said, the locket's old. He gave it to a niece as an engagement gift, but it wasn't really for her. Those letters aren't her initials. Anyway, she didn't have it one week before she tripped trying to beat a cable car to the corner. The cable car ran over her leg, and it had to be amputated above the knee. That sort of killed the wedding. Her man ran off, and she never married."

"That's an awful story," Debra said. "I'm so sorry."

"What comes next ain't no better." The woman unzipped her coat as if she were warm. "That girl never sold the locket. I guess she kept it because of the wedding thing. Her niece found the locket when they were going through belongings after her death. And you know how girls can be. That niece claimed the locket and took to wearing it, even though the letters didn't fit her either."

"Would you like a cup of tea?" Debra asked.

"Coffee, if you have it."

"All I have is instant."

"I'm not choosy."

While Debra fixed a cup of instant coffee, the woman continued her story.

"The niece wore the locket for maybe a month before she came down with the flu. It was right before Christmas. She didn't live to see the new year."

Debra handed the woman the coffee, and the woman immediately sipped it despite the heat.

"Thanks," the woman said. "Coffee is the best thing ever."

"Go on with your story," Debra said. "What happened next?"

"That locket stayed in the niece's bureau for a time. Years. It was sort of hidden, I guess. Anyway, they gave the bureau to my mother who went about trying to bring it back to life, so to speak. She found the box, that box, and that locket. My mother's heart jumped out of her chest when she saw it. It's so pretty."

The woman wrapped both hands around the cup, warming herself.

"My mother never wore the locket. She put it in her little china chest so everyone could see it. She would touch it sometimes like it was special. I guess it was. It wasn't a year later that my dad ran off with a waitress at the diner. Just didn't come home one day. Took all the money and disappeared. I still don't know where he is. Not that it matters. I wouldn't have anything to do with him anyway."

"That's awful," Debra said.

"It doesn't get any better. You can imagine what happened after Dad left. Mom couldn't find a good job, and there were bills, lots of bills. Over time, everything disappeared. We kept moving, always down. All the nice things disappeared somehow and yet, no matter how bad things got, Mom never sold the locket. Even when she slipped on the ice and broke her hip, she didn't even think of selling it. And she made me promise not to sell it either. When Mom couldn't move, she got pneumonia. That's bad. I didn't catch it in time."

"How long have you been on the street?"

"Too long. I have to get away before it kills me. Oak Butt will kill me."

"Then why are you selling the locket, if I may ask?"

"Because it's all I have, and I think it's cursed. No one in my family has ever had a lick of luck with it. If I can get a few bucks out of the deal, I'll take it."

Debra stared at the locket, not quite sure what to do.

"The last train will be leaving in a bit," the woman said. "I'd like to be on it."

Debra stared at the locket. "Let's get you on that train."

***

The last thing Debra did before she left was to take one last look at the locket. It spoke to her in ways she couldn't quite explain. She was certain that she didn't believe everything the woman had said. Debra guessed that the story had been embellished for her benefit, but that didn't matter. The locket was special. Debra believed that. The locket was very special.

Walking to her car, Debra performed her due diligence. She checked the benches and the escalators. They were empty. That brought a smile to Debra's face. She found the snow actually charming in some fashion. It made her glad for Christmas, for her sales. It had been a good day … snow, sales, a locket, and no weeping girl.

In bed, Debra said a small prayer for the woman who had sold the locket. Debra wanted the woman to find a good life, no matter where it was.

***

It wasn't until the next morning that Debra felt a bit out of sorts.

The Christmas rush was no time to be sick.

Debra trudged through the new fallen snow, her head beginning to ache. No one-shoed girl was around, and Debra was not surprised. It had been a while since the weeping girl had made an appearance. Debra had come to feel confident that she was no longer in hallucination mode. That was a good thing. Debra wasn't at all sure she could make her store a success if she had to worry about seeing things.

Throughout the busy day, Debra's condition worsened. Fever billowed up inside her. The tiny headache marched along, getting larger with every passing hour. She asked herself more than once just why illness came equipped with aches and pains. Wasn't fever and headache enough? Luckily, Debra did not lack for hot tea. She sipped tea all day because she didn't trust the cold medications some people recommended. She had the feeling that cold remedies dulled the mind, just when she needed all the thinking she could muster.

By the end of the day, Debra was not only feverish but dizzy. She looked forward to the closing time. When the store emptied, she smiled and started around the counter. What was thirty minutes at this time of day? She would lock the door and pray for a good night.

Debra rounded the counter and stopped dead.

She stopped even as the weeping girl raised her head.

Debra thought the girl's face couldn't be real.

Because it was bloody. And bruised—and battered. With one eye closed, and one lip swollen.

If the beaten girl tried to say something, Debra never knew. She dropped her cup of tea and collapsed.

Chapter 7

When Debra woke, the weeping girl's face flashed in her memory. Debra quickly looked around the store. It was empty. She climbed to her knees and faced the spilled tea. The tea was cold. Luckily, the plastic mug hadn't broken. Fighting her spinning head, she cleaned the spill and locked the front door. She wanted to go home, but she didn't feel well enough, not yet. She returned to her tea kettle and prepared another cup. Hands shaking, quivering with fever, Debra sat and tried to reason through the vision she had experienced. Where had the face come from? Debra had never seen that before. How had her addled brain created that?

It had to be her brain.

That much seemed obvious. Because if it wasn't her brain …

Her head hurt too much to keep thinking. She needed to get home. She needed a hot soak in the tub and some of those drugs she hadn't taken all day. She simply couldn't keep thinking. She sleepwalked through the closing of the store, and if she checked out the benches and escalators on the way to the car, she didn't remember. In fact, she didn't remember driving home. Luckily, it was one of those routines that she had added to her habits. One minute she was on the road and the next, she was running hot water for her soak. Had she not been sick, she might have acknowledged the fear slipping through her veins. She might have spent some hours trying to make sense of the battered girl. But she wasn't well, and the meds quelled the headache and pains, the wine shut down her brain, and the steaming water filled her with a warmth that promised healing. She didn't remember getting into bed or falling asleep.

Time disappeared.

She woke in the morning, and her head felt clear.

She didn't even remember the girl … until the tea kettle whistled. That was when Debra stopped short and recalled the face. That was when she looked around for the weeping girl. That was when she felt the presence of … whatever the girl was.

A figment of her imagination.

Debra pulled her mind together and made tea. She remembered that she hadn't updated her books the night before, and that would have to wait because she didn't have the time. At least she'd felt good enough to open the store. That was something. As she carried the tea to her bedroom, she looked about nervously. She was pretty sure that the porcelain cup in her hand would shatter if she dropped it like a scared little girl. If she didn't have time to update her books, she didn't have time to clean up spilled tea.

***

Debra opened her shop with a bit of trepidation. Would the weeping, battered girl be there? Debra had no desire to bump into the girl a second time. Well, in Debra's case, she had no desire to allow her brain to dream up another image. As she went about her morning routine, she kept an eye out. That she felt better gave her some assurance. No fever would stoke the fire of her imagination. She saw no one. That, by itself, made her feel better.

By the end of the day, Debra felt like herself—mostly. The remnants of her short illness still roamed her body, but she had survived the day. She hurried home, mindful of the empty benches and escalators. She knew she would never be able to walk through the station without looking for the girl. It had become … routine.

Christmas rose like a mountain before Debra. Her shop was doing well, and she was happy. She looked forward to a day without work, a chance to catch up on some tasks at the house. Work didn't disappear because she didn't have the time to do it. What Debra had come to understand was the power of the locket. It seemed that every visitor somehow wandered up to the counter and paused to study the locket. Some asked to see the locket. A few offered to buy it, but Debra didn't feel that selling the locket was a good thing. She considered the locket one of her better investments, as it drew in buyers. If she sold it, she didn't think her store would have as much appeal.

It was one of her customers who suggested that Debra get the locket appraised for insurance purposes. Should it be lost or stolen or consumed by fire, Debra would need money to replace it—if it could be replaced. So, on a chilly day, she added the locket and its raggedy box to her purse and took the train into town during an extended lunch hour. She needed to discover just how valuable the locket was.

"This is old, but not so very old," the old jeweler said as he examined the locket. "I mean, it's not like something from the middle ages."

"Can you tell me anything about it?" Debra asked.

"Two things. The initials on the inside are probably the initials of the person who bought the locket. And that person bought the locket from S&K jewelers sometime before 1933."

Debra was surprised. "How do you know that?"

"In the old days, jewelry makers and sellers often added their initials to a piece." He turned the locket so Debra could see the bottom and some very tiny etching there. "It was for identification purposes and mostly invisible unless looked for. S&K was a rather expensive shop that did well until the Depression. If I remember my history, it burned to the ground in 1933."

"That's amazing. And the initials?"

"I'm afraid I have no way of ascertaining whose locket this was. All the records disappeared in the fire. Would you like a new box for it?"

"No," Debra answered. "The old box feels right if you know what I mean."

"Indeed, I do."

Debra was thinking about the locket as she rode the train back to Oak Bottom. Who had purchased the locket? How had it gotten into the hands of some distant uncle who presented it as a wedding gift? The jeweler had assured Debra that, while the locket was certainly valuable, it was not some sort of heirloom or museum piece. Should it disappear, he assured her he could fashion a replica if she wished. She didn't wish. The locket was practically perfect the way it was. If lost, it would remain lost. As the train approached Oak Bottom, Debra realized that the car was empty.

Odd.

Debra had expected a busy car this close to Christmas, and yet, she was the only passenger. She looked about … and froze.

Ahead, on her right, Debra spotted two feet on the floor. No, not two feet. One shoe and one wrinkled sock. While there was no head visible, the shoe and sock clearly showed. A shiver ran up Debra's spine. The button shoe looked terribly familiar. The sock matched the one she remembered. Debra knew, deep inside, that the shoe and sock belonged to the weeping, battered girl. They could belong to no one else.

Debra shook, literally shook, as she stared at the unmoving feet. It wasn't enough that she had seen the girl on the station platforms and inside the store; now Debra was seeing things on the train.

Terrifying.

"No, no, no, no," Debra said softly, hoping that sheer denial would do away with the shoe and sock. But the shoe remained buttoned, the sock wrinkled. She squeezed the purse in her lap and stared. How could her brain fail to work?

Debra knew there was only one course of action. She didn't really have a choice. She had to confront the girl. Debra had to find out once and for all just how addled her brain was. To sit and do nothing was to acquiesce to the faulty parts of her mind. Shaking, biting her lip, Debra pulled herself erect. She still could see nothing but the shoe and the sock. That unnerved her, and she started to sink back into her seat.

No!

She was committed to learning more about … about …

She stepped into the aisle and grabbed the seat ahead of her. She pulled herself slowly ahead, half expecting the girl to suddenly rise up and let out some wicked scream. Debra froze once, unable to continue. But she overcame the numbing fear and pushed ahead until she was directly behind the seat she needed to see. At that moment, she felt as if she were a child again, a child staring at a closet door, afraid to open it because something evil and wicked waited behind the door. There was no reason to believe that something wicked waited. But reason had no power against fear. Fear was primal; reason was a construct—or so she had been told. Steeling herself against the battered face she expected to see, Debra quickly stepped ahead and turned.

Chapter 8

The seat was empty, totally empty. No weeping, no battered girl, no shoe or sock, just empty.

Debra could hardly believe her eyes. She stared and then sat in the seat as if the girl was merely invisible. Debra, and no one else occupied the seat. Debra stared, not able to quite understand. The shoe and sock had been real, totally real.

Or had it?

When the train stopped, Debra fairly ran off the train. She didn't look back, and she didn't stop until she was back in her shop. She was still shaking. She would have kept shaking had the store not filled with shoppers. Business and money were maybe the only things that could drive the weeping girl from Debra's mind. She became far too busy to worry about the girl that wasn't there. Debra showed the locket a few times. She chatted and smiled and pushed the girl out of her brain. People came and went. Debra managed to reach the end of the day without feeling that eerie fear she had experienced in the train car. It was only as Debra locked the door that she remembered the girl. What about the weeping girl?

Debra went to her back room and sat for a moment. She had reached a kind of crisis. She had seen the weeping girl in various places around the station and train. Debra had not determined if the girl was somehow real, as she knew that was improbable or something manufactured by Debra's mind, which was more likely. If the girl were some kind of vision, then Debra had a big problem. If the girl was in some fashion real, that presented another issue. Because if the weeping girl was real, she wasn't of this earth. No human could appear and disappear at will. No human could move as fast as the girl. If the girl were real, then she existed on some plane Debra didn't recognize.

But Debra didn't want to believe that she could fashion the weeping girl from whole cloth. The girl matched none of Debra's childhood memories or fears. The girl came from no book Debra had ever read. Debra was simply flabbergasted by the details of the weeping girl. Nothing in Debra's past pointed to the girl, nothing. Was Debra going slowly insane?

She looked at her shaking hands and wondered how she might determine if the girl were real. Debra didn't have an easy or immediate answer. And yet, she knew she couldn't go on the way she was going. Fear and the accompanying doubt had curtailed her appetite. She wasn't sleeping as well as she should. She was pretty sure she could make it to New Year's, but after that? She didn't know how much longer or harder she could push.

But how to find the truth?

Was she the only person who could see the weeping girl? Was Debra the only one who experienced the battered face? If she wasn't, who else had met the girl? And how would Debra meet the others who had seen what Debra had seen? She was at the end of her wits. Was she totally alone? Was she a majority of one? She rubbed her temples, trying to figure out her next move. For one laughable moment, she wondered if she should just sleep in the back room. If she didn't walk to her car … no, she had met the battered girl in the shop. Sleeping in the store guaranteed nothing. In fact, Debra would probably be far safer at home. Deciding nothing, she pushed herself up and began her closing routine, a routine that allowed only part of her mind to consider her problem.

Trudging to her car, Debra kept a sharp eye out for the weeping girl. Debra wished, despite her fears, that she could talk to the weeping girl. If they could … communicate, then Debra could at least determine if her own brain was working. If the girl kept disappearing, then how might Debra gauge her own sanity? Trying to determine if she was crazy was driving her crazy.

At home, Debra forced the girl from her mind. With deliberate focus, Debra brought her books up to date. She was pleased. She had made more money than she had thought possible. That called for another glass of wine, which she relished. For the first time in a month, Debra simply did nothing. She plopped into a chair and looked out her back window at the snow-filled yard. A full moon made the snow glisten, as pretty as Debra could remember. For a moment, a second, she thought she saw the girl. Debra sat bolt upright and stared.

No, no, no girl.

A shadow, a tree shadow, nothing more.

Debra shivered, suddenly aware that her life would never be smooth sailing as long as she didn't trust her own brain. Some way, somehow, she needed to reach some resolution. She had to know. She had to find resolution. Otherwise, she would never find peace.

And she needed peace.

***

There were police cars with lights flashing when Debra arrived the next morning. Her usual space was not available, and she was forced to park in a new spot. As she walked past the police cruisers, she stopped. One of the railroad security officers was standing to the side.

Debra stopped. "What happened?"

"Drunk or something. Slammed on the brakes and hit a light pole. Claims there was a girl right in front of him, but there wasn't anything."

"How do you know that?"

"No footprints. No one can get to the middle of the lot without leaving prints. That would take a fairy or something."

"What did the girl look like?" Debra asked. "Was she wearing one shoe?"

"There was no girl. That's the point. Drunks are always seeing things."

Debra thought a moment. "I'm Debra." She held out her hand.

"Tony. Nice to meet you." He flashed her a dazzling smile.

"Tony, you know … well, I see this young girl, in her teens, that regularly rides the train. I see her in the morning and then at night. She always looks scared, like she's lost. I'd like to meet her. She's always alone and always looks so sad. Do you know her name or maybe her family?"

Debra was sure Tony knew who she was talking about, but the puzzled look on his face started to worry her. *What if I am crazy?*

Tony stared at Debra with confusion. "Ma'am, I have been working in the station for years now and there is no passenger that fits that description. Are you sure it's the same girl?"

An embarrassed Debra stood frozen in fear. *I must be crazy. Surely I can't be imagining this.*

"You know … I'm not sure. Well, thanks, Tony, nice officially meeting you. Oh, is there anyone else who's been working here a lot longer?" She crossed her fingers. Surely someone had seen the girl.

"Yeah, Ernie. He's worked here forever."

"Where might I find him?"

Tony gave her a strange look. "He'll be at his retirement party Thursday, around noon. That's his last day."

"I need to talk to him."

"Then come to the party, Bill's Tavern. If Ernie doesn't drink too much, you might just understand him." He flashed Debra his dazzling smile again, but Debra didn't notice.

Tony shrugged, then laughed as he moved toward a waving policeman. Debra watched him walk away. If Tony had never seen her, then was she losing her mind? She hurried away, entered the station and turned toward her shop.

And there she was. The girl that didn't exist. The girl that no one ever saw except Debra. The scream involuntarily escaped her mouth, and Tony ran over to her.

"Debra?"

She turned to look at Tony and then quickly turned back while pointing at the girl. "Here's the girl I was asking about. Do you know her?"

Tony raised an eyebrow as he looked where Debra was pointing. The girl was gone. And she knew Tony thought she was crazy.

"Never mind, Tony, it was just a shadow."

He shrugged and left.

Chapter 9

Debra stopped, just stopped dead. She had taken the train to work, desperately wanting to see the girl; to know she hadn't lost her mind. But the girl hadn't been on the train.

But here, halfway between her and the shop was the bench, and on the bench was the weeping girl. There was no mistaking the girl. Coat, shoe, sock, and lank hair. Debra had become familiar with the details. She knew the girl, well, knew what the girl looked like. And even though Debra couldn't hear the girl, she knew the girl was crying. The girl always cried. Debra knew the girl's face was battered, too. She knew, and yet, she still didn't know. Debra didn't know if she could trust her eyes or her ears.

Debra took a step, and the weeping girl vanished.

The effect startled Debra, even though she half expected it. The disappearance was like turning off a television—here a second ago, now gone. Shaking her head, Debra pressed on. She didn't expect to see the girl again. Debra was correct. The one-shoe girl was totally gone.

Morning turned into evening, and Debra stayed late to restock the shelves.
She went into the back room to sit down and promptly fell asleep.

She awoke with a start, gasping as she looked at her watch. The train! She had to leave now. She ran toward the escalator and boarded the train with only minutes to spare. Darkness made the train station creepy, and Debra didn't need any more creepy.

As she glanced out the window, she saw the girl. "Help me!" Debra felt the words more than heard them.

"Who is that girl?" she asked the man sitting a seat in front of her and pointed towards the darkness.

"What girl?"

She was gone. "Never mind. Sorry to bother you."

When Debra's stop arrived, she smiled at the conductor before a gripping fear overtook her. She did not like having to walk the block to her place at night, fearful that the girl would appear. And she did.

"Help me," she said again. "I'm lost."

"Who are you?" Debra asked, her voice shaking. "Where do you live?"

"I don't live. He killed me!" A gut-wrenching sob welled up and escaped her mouth.

"Who? What?" Debra couldn't get the words out. "Let me help you."

Debra reached for the girl's hand, but there was nothing to grasp on to. Debra shut her eyes. *Please, someone, help me! I can't be crazy! She's real; she has to be.*

When she opened her eyes, the girl was gone. This time, it was from Debra's mouth that the gut-wrenching sob escaped.

***

Thursday morning passed with tea and customers. The fresh snow seemed to stimulate the shoppers who were more than happy to spend money. Debra sold the Santas, elves, and wooden Christmas trees, and by noon, she thought the shelves were beginning to look a bit bare. That was too bad since she had no additional inventory in the back room. It seemed like a good problem to have. She was considering how she might acquire a bit more when she remembered Ernie, the retiring security officer. She managed to shoo out the last few customers. Locking the door, Debra almost ran to the restaurant—but she didn't forget to look for the weeping girl.

Who wasn't there.

When Debra entered the restaurant, she spotted the retirement party. Perhaps twenty people sat in a private room. At the head of the table stood a man Debra didn't recognize. She supposed he was Ernie, and he looked more than old enough for retirement.

Red-faced and smiling, he looked as happy as Debra wished she could be. For a moment, Debra felt a pang of regret. Since she had opened her shop, she couldn't see a time when she might be able to retire. In fact, Debra didn't see a time when she would wish to retire. Work was good, and good work kept a person young. Or so Debra had always been told. As she watched, Ernie told a few more jokes and sat down. Debra knew she couldn't hang around all afternoon. Before the cake was brought in, Debra moved to Ernie and tapped his shoulder.

"Hello," Ernie said. "You're the owner of the shop."

"Yes," Debra smiled. "And I have a favor to ask."

"I'm retired," he said. "But I'll do what I can."

"Before you leave today, could you stop by my store?"

"I suppose so. Any particular reason?"

"Just something I want to clear up, about a certain person."

Ernie's look told Debra that maybe, just maybe, he knew what she was talking about.

"Please," Debra said. "You may be the only one who knows the answer."

"Sure," Ernie said. "I'll make a note of it."

"Thank you so much."

Debra hurried away before Ernie could ask a question or change his mind. On her way back, she checked the benches.

No weeping girl.

Debra began the afternoon with the hope that Ernie knew something, anything about the girl. If he didn't …

Debra didn't want to be the only person who ever saw the girl. That would be disastrous.

Darkness wasn't far away when the bell over the door jangled. Debra looked up from the woman who was examining the locket. At the door stood Ernie, and his face was even redder than it had been at lunch. He looked about the shop. Debra hoped Ernie was in a condition to answer questions. As she looked, Ernie waved and smiled. At least he hadn't forgotten her.

It was ten more minutes before Debra had the opportunity to talk to Ernie, who came to the counter where his eyes immediately found the locket. Every visitor found the locket.

"Damn pretty," Ernie said. "Looks old."

"It is," Debra said. "I was lucky to acquire it."

"Well, what's on your mind? I have to leave in a bit."

"I'd buy you a drink if I could," Debra said. "Because I have a rather odd request."

"I've heard most of the oddest. I hope I can help."

"It's about … this isn't easy to say. It's about a girl, a girl I see around the station."

Ernie rubbed his nose and closed one eye. "I sort of figured that's what you wanted to know about."

"You've seen her? The girl with the lank hair and one shoe?"

"If you're around here long enough, you'll see her."

Debra felt a surge of joy. She wasn't crazy. If Ernie had seen the weeping girl, then Debra had, at least, one other fellow traveler.

"What do you know about her?" Debra asked.

"Not a lot, stories mostly."

"Tell me."

"It goes something like this, and don't quote me. I imagine a lot of truth has been lost over the years. People make up stuff to fill in the gaps if you know what I mean."

"I'll take it with a grain of salt."

"Several grains. Because the story about the girl goes back a hundred years or so. That was when the line to Oak Bottom was brand-new. There were half a dozen houses out this way, and this was the end of the line. The girl, I don't know her name, lived in Oak Bottom and traveled to the city on the train. Lots of young girls worked as servants in those days. She was one of them. One night not long before

Christmas, the girl was coming home. Most nights, she was alone on her return, but not this night. Because she never made it home. They found her body by the side of the tracks. She had been beaten and tossed off the train. No purse, no ID; she was just a broken young girl."

"That's awful."

"Legend is the girl is looking for her purse or whatever she had that night. People see her on the train, going in and coming out. On the benches, too, and platform. She's not there all the time. I think I spot her most around Christmas. She must have died about then. At least, that's what I think."

"But she never causes a problem?"

"No, just scares people when she disappears. But not many people see her. I guess she likes you."

Debra laughed. "I wouldn't call it exactly that."

"Yeah, I know. The first time I saw her, I freaked. None of the other guys ever saw her. I thought I was going nuts."

Debra talked to Ernie for a few more minutes. They compared sightings and details, and Debra was sure that Ernie had seen the weeping girl. When Ernie left, Debra felt balanced for the first time in weeks. She was sane. Well, as sane as any person who just happened to spot a ghost once in a while could be. Debra was certain that from now on, she would be able to handle weeping girl, who wasn't a threat in any way.

That night, as she headed for her car, she still checked the benches and escalators.

No weeping girl.

And that didn't bother Debra at all. As she drove home, she sang a Christmas carol. Her poor voice didn't bother her; nothing could bother her now.

Epilogue

The day after Christmas was lonely for Debra. The shop was empty. That was fine. It gave Debra a chance to clean up and rearrange. She had ordered replacement inventory, but it had not yet arrived. She kept busy, and the last thing she wanted to polish was the locket. She pulled it from the case and set it on the countertop. Feeling inquisitive, she opened the locket and read the initials. For some reason, they spoke to her. She wondered what girl had had the engraving done. Who had gone to the trouble?

She looked up and froze.

A few feet away stood the weeping girl, her face battered and bloody. Lank hair, a single shoe, and a worn coat. A shiver ran halfway up Debra's spine and then stopped. Debra wasn't scared, not really. The young girl wasn't dangerous. She was just lost. She stared ahead, and Debra had the idea that the girl saw something; something that was important to her. What was it?

Debra looked from the weeping girl to the locket and something dawned on her.

The locket?

Debra had no idea how or why the locket mattered. It probably didn't. But the locket was all Debra had. If it didn't make a difference … then what would?

Debra held up the locket so the weeping girl could see it. But she had stopped crying.

"My locket …" The girl smiled and held out her hand. "Please?"

"It's yours?"

The girl nodded, and Debra understood. "Did the man take this from you?"

"He took everything from me."

Debra felt her pain and gently placed the locket in the girl's hand. "Not this."

The girl smiled at her. "I'm Emily." Then she vanished.

The End

More Books by Carrie Bates

The Haunting of Thomas House

The Haunting of Maple Mansion

The Haunting of Hilltop Mansion

The Haunting of Whitfield Mansion

The Haunting of Owensboro Mansion

The Haunting of Maynard Mansion

The Haunting of Kessinger Mansion

The Haunting of Krakow Convent

The Haunting of St. Doyle Seminary

The Haunting of Skye Ocean Liner

The Haunting of Harper House

The Haunting of Mansfield Mansion

The Haunting of Cardon House

The Haunting of Bertha House

The Haunting of McGregor Mansion

The Haunting of Redding House

The Haunting of Barrister Mansion

The Haunting of Wescott House

The Haunting of Macklen House

The Haunting of Brantura House

The Haunting of Langdon House

The Haunting of Mercer House

The Haunting of Camp Lakewood

A Christmas Haunting: Clark Mansion

The Haunting of Bella Lucia's

Printed in Great Britain
by Amazon